Just Custard

Joe Hackett and
Alexandra Colombo

Evans

All Duncan would eat was custard.
Just cold custard.
On its own.
From a tin.

Duncan didn't use a spoon. He drank
the custard with a big red stripy straw.
He slurped it between his teeth.

Slurp,
Slurp!

Dad took the straw away, and got quite cross.

"You're seven years old. Stop messing about," he said. "Custard isn't enough to live on."

7

Sitting in Mum's lap, drinking a bottle of milk, was Duncan's new baby sister, Angela. She was only a few months old.

"She's a little angel. That's why we've called her Angela," Mum told anyone who would listen.

At school, Duncan didn't eat his lunch, even though it looked delicious. He demanded custard in a tin.

11

Miss James asked to see Duncan alone,
and talked quietly to him.

He sat in her special armchair.

"Is there anything worrying you,
Duncan?" she asked.

Duncan thought for a minute.

"Yes, but it's a secret," he said, and he whispered something in her ear.

"Right," she said. "Let's see what we can do about that."

13

That night, at home, Duncan would still
only eat custard.

Dad was so cross that he sent
Duncan to his bedroom.

"It's not fair!" shouted Duncan. He
climbed out of his bedroom window, slid
down the drainpipe and ran to the park
to play football with his friends.

But his friends weren't there and it was
starting to get dark.

Duncan didn't want to go home, so he
found a bench, curled up and tried to go
to sleep.

16

17

Suddenly, he heard the crunch of stones underfoot. A torch beam swept backwards and forwards in the darkness, casting shadows. A man wearing a yellow coat came closer and closer.

Duncan was terrified and froze to the bench.

He screamed.

"Duncan!" shouted Dad. "Thank goodness I've found you!"

He scooped Duncan up and gave him a big cuddle. "Let's get you home, we've been so worried."

21

The next morning, Mum went to see
Miss James. Mum sat in her special
armchair and they had a long talk.

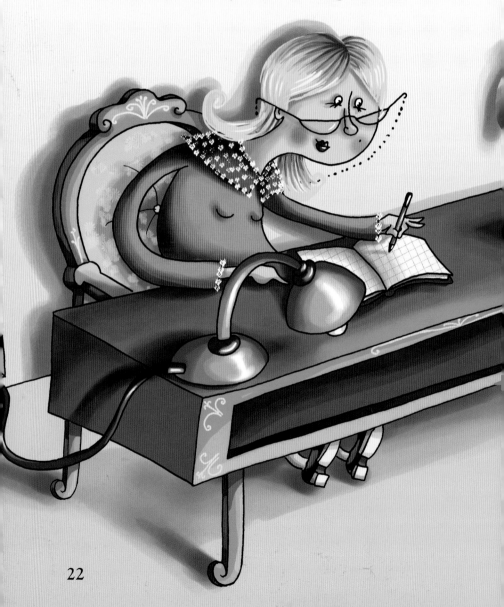

23

When Duncan came home from school, Mum said, "Do you think Angela might like custard too? She should be ready for something different from milk by now. Would you like to feed her?"

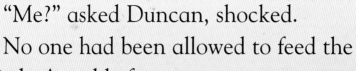

"Me?" asked Duncan, shocked.

No one had been allowed to feed the
Little Angel before.

25

Duncan dipped a plastic spoon into a
pot of baby custard, and offered it
to Angela.

She opened her mouth and he popped it in. He offered her another spoonful and she ate that, too. She carried on until she had finished the whole pot!

Custard

The Little Angel grinned at him, her
smile covered in custard.
  "She likes you, you know," Mum said.
Duncan was very, very pleased.

That night, it was chicken, peas and baked potato for tea. Afterwards, there was chocolate pudding – Duncan's favourite!

Duncan ate all his food without even
being asked.

"Will you want some custard with
your pudding, son?" Dad asked.

"No, thanks, Dad. Custard is just for
babies!" Duncan laughed.

3

Why not try reading another **Spirals** book?

Megan's Tick Tock Rocket by Andrew Fusek Peters, Polly Peters
HB: 978 0237 53348 0 PB: 978 0237 53342 7

Growl! by Vivian French
HB: 978 0237 53351 0 PB: 978 0237 53345 8

John and the River Monster by Paul Harrison
HB: 978 0237 53350 2 PB: 978 0237 53344 1

Froggy Went a Hopping by Alan Durant
HB: 978 0237 53352 9 PB: 978 0237 53346 5

Amy's Slippers by Mary Chapman
HB: 978 0237 53353 3 PB: 978 0237 53347 2

The Flamingo Who Forgot by Alan Durant
HB: 978 0237 53349 6 PB: 978 0237 53343 4

Glub! by Penny Little
HB: 978 0237 53462 2 PB: 978 0237 53461 5

The Grumpy Queen by Valerie Wilding
HB: 978 0237 53460 8 PB: 978 0237 53459 2

Happy by Mara Bergman
HB: 978 0237 53532 2 PB: 978 0237 53536 0

Sink or Swim by Dereen Taylor
HB: 978 0237 53531 5 PB: 978 0237 53535 3

Sophie's Timepiece by Mary Chapman
HB: 978 0237 53530 8 PB: 978 0237 53534 6

The Perfect Prince by Paul Harrison
HB: 978 0237 53533 9 PB: 978 0237 53537 7

Tuva by Mick Gowar
HB: 978 0237 53879 8 PB: 978 0237 53885 9

Wait a Minute, Ruby! by Mary Chapman
HB: 978 0237 53882 8 PB: 978 0237 53888 0

George and the Dragonfly by Andy Blackford
HB: 978 0237 53878 1 PB: 978 0237 53884 2

Monster in the Garden by Anne Rooney
HB: 978 0237 53883 5 PB: 978 0237 53889 7

Just Custard by Joe Hackett
HB: 978 0237 53881 1 PB: 978 0237 53887 3

The King of Kites by Judith Heneghan
HB: 978 0237 53880 4 PB: 978 0237 53886 6